BEYOND
BASKETBALL

BY JAKE MADDOX

text by
Joelle Wisler

STONE ARCH BOOKS
a capstone imprint

Jake Maddox JV Girls books are published by
Stone Arch Books
a Capstone imprint
1710 Roe Crest Drive
North Mankato, Minnesota 56003
www.mycapstone.com

Copyright © 2019 Stone Arch Books

Cataloging-in-Publication Data is available on the Library of Congress website.
ISBN: 978-1-4965-6343-9 (library binding)
ISBN: 978-1-4965-6345-3 (paperback)
ISBN: 978-1-4965-6347-7 (eBook PDF)

Summary: Juniper is the Panthers' tallest player and the daughter of the coach, but she doesn't
know if she is interested enough in basketball to put her heart into the game.

Editor: Nate LeBoutillier
Designer: Tori Abraham

Image Credits: Shutterstock: Brocreative, back cover, chapter openers, cluckva, 92–95 (background),
Eky Studio, throughout (stripes design), Monkey Business Images, cover

Printed and bound in the United States of America.
PA021

TABLE OF CONTENTS

CHAPTER 1

UNDER PRESSURE

Juniper Jackson stood at the free throw line, her palms slick with sweat. The crowd in her school's gymnasium was silent, waiting. The Panthers and Eagles were tied up with only eighteen seconds left on the clock. It was up to her.

In the corner of her eye, Juniper saw her dad pacing back and forth with his clipboard. She could practically hear him holding his breath. Her stomach churned.

She bounced the ball once, twice. Juniper looked around at all of the other players. Her teammates, the Panthers, wore uniforms that were navy. The visiting Eagles wore clashing red.

The girl who'd shoved her glared daggers at Juniper from her spot on the lane. Just one more foul and she'd be warming the bench. Juniper wasn't sure how that was *her* fault.

Juniper took in a deep breath, bent her right elbow, and then lobbed the ball up into the air. It arced down with a slow motion backspin and . . . completely missed the basket.

The crowd groaned.

"C'mon Juniper, you can do better than that!" her dad shouted.

Juniper felt shame rush through her. Her cheeks turned the color of the Eagles' uniforms. She felt like a giant standing out there. Her most recent growth spurt had probably put her over six feet tall.

She didn't know for sure. She was too afraid to get measured.

Standing at the free throw line, Juniper felt like the tallest twelve-year-old in the whole world. She could feel everyone's eyes on her. They stared at her freakishly long arms and legs. They stared at her string-bean torso. They waited to see what she would do.

The ref tossed the ball to Juniper. She caught it one-handed, feeling the slap of the leather like an electric shock.

Juniper bounced the ball but had trouble concentrating. She rushed the shot, anxious to have her moment in the spotlight be over with. The ball hit the top left corner of the square on the backboard, clipped the rim, and bounced out.

Juniper stood there, stunned. She was upset she'd missed. And she knew her dad would be disappointed in her.

The Eagles rebounded the ball.

Mila, the Panthers point guard, lunged for the ball, trying for a steal. She rammed her elbow into the ribcage of the Eagles forward, knocking her to the ground.

The ref blew her whistle. Foul. The Eagles would get free throws.

"Timeout!" Juniper's dad shouted, his face going purple. He slammed his clipboard down on the bench.

The Panthers players all looked at each other warily. Their coach was really angry. The girls huddled around him.

"This is what we're going to do," he said. He picked up his clipboard and jabbed his dry erase marker around to show his Panthers players the strategy. After explaining, he stared pointedly at Juniper. "Looks like we'll need to spend some extra time on free throws this week," he said.

Juniper wished she were smaller. Her head towered above everyone else's. She kept her eyes glued to the scuffed toes of her basketball shoes.

Her dad normally didn't call her out like that in front of the other players. Normally, he was kinder and more patient with *all* of their mistakes. She especially felt embarrassed that he was paying extra attention to her.

The girls jogged back out onto the court.

"Nice choke," Veronica, the Panthers forward, said to Juniper.

Juniper didn't have time to think about Veronica's cruel comment. She had to get her hands on that ball. They lined up around the lane under the Eagles basket.

The blond Eagles forward spun the ball in her hands and then let it settle into her palm. She bent and straightened her elbow, and the ball flew up and up, sliding seamlessly into the net. A perfect shot.

The Panthers were now down by one.

The next shot came up short. Veronica grabbed the rebound and passed to Mila.

Just ten seconds left, and the Panthers were out of timeouts and quickly running out of time. Juniper hustled down the court, pumping her arms and legs as fast as she could to keep up with Mila.

Eight seconds.

Juniper could hear the crowd cheering and counting down the final seconds.

Seven . . . six . . . five . . .

Juniper's long legs brought her underneath the basket. She was alone.

Mila found her and passed. The ball flew like an arrow into Juniper's waiting hands. Juniper stared up at the easiest shot in the world. She could taste the victory.

Three seconds . . . two seconds.

Juniper's dad's voice boomed, "Shoot it!"

Juniper gathered herself under the basket, the ball heavy and light at the same time. She felt as if she was underwater. Time slowed. It was just her, the ball, and the basket. Nothing else existed.

Juniper shot the ball. It went up . . . up . . . and then it kept going. She'd angled it too high. It smacked the top of the board with too much force and bounced off without even grazing the rim. The buzzer went off.

Juniper squatted down and held her head in her hands.

The home crowd went silent. The visiting team's cheers echoed in the gym. The Eagles danced and hugged each other in celebration.

Her heart heavy, Juniper stood up to go shake hands, to be a good sport. She couldn't even look at her dad.

"It's okay, Juniper," Mila said. She patted Juniper's back as they headed to the locker room.

Juniper smiled sadly down at her small friend with the curly blond hair. Mila's small size always made Juniper feel even more enormous than usual.

"Thanks, Mila," Juniper said. She was thankful for having a good friend on her team, even if she was a shrimp. "That was an awesome pass."

Juniper took a longer shower than normal. She dawdled while packing up her sweaty uniform. She knew that when she was done she'd have to face her dad. Finally, she realized she couldn't hide in the locker room forever. She slung her duffel bag over her shoulder, sighed, and pushed open the door.

Her dad was sitting in the bleachers. He tossed a basketball between his large hands. Juniper couldn't read his emotions. His face was a closed-off mask.

"Hey, Dad," Juniper said. "I'm sorry. I know I need to work on my free throws."

"Yep," he said, tossing the ball at her. "And you're going to start right now."

"What?" Juniper said, startled.

It was late. She had school the next day. She still had homework to do.

He had started walking away and turned back to say, "The only way you're going to improve is if you practice. So you'll practice. I'll be in my office. I'll come and get you in an hour."

Juniper rolled the ball around in her hands. Tears threatened to make an escape. She'd tried. She really had.

The locker-room door opened. Veronica stepped out and sneered at Juniper. "Wow," she said, "a double choke. I didn't even know that was possible."

Juniper turned away, gritted her teeth, and started shooting.

CHAPTER 2

CHOOSING HOOPS

It was Saturday. Juniper sat at her desk, looking through a physics book. She marveled at the equations and numbers that could somehow describe the whole world. Soft and relaxing music played on her speakers, like always. Her heart felt quiet and free from thoughts of basketball and missed shots.

Juniper's sister, Rose, was home from college. She lounged on Juniper's floral bedspread.

Rose tossed a basketball from one hand to the other. The slapping sound of the ball comforted both sisters. "Sorry I missed your game, Shorty," she said.

Juniper rolled her eyes and spun her desk chair around. Rose was actually shorter than Juniper by an inch or two. And counting.

"You didn't miss much," Juniper said. "I totally choked. And Dad was *not* happy with me."

"Oh yeah? He was always rough on me too," Rose said. "But only because he cared." Rose made air quotes with her fingers around the word *cared*.

Juniper snorted.

"Just try to make it through the year without quitting or hating him too much," Rose said. She sat up in the bed and tossed the ball to Juniper.

Juniper caught it and passed it back.

"You're tough," said Rose. "You'll make it."

The girls heard the sound of their father's feet clomping down the hallway.

Rose hopped up from the bed. "I'll check you later, Shorty," she said. "Have fun doing the million drills I'm sure Dad has planned for you today."

Juniper groaned. Rose took the ball and faked a pass at Juniper and then at their dad as he stepped into Juniper's doorway. His enormous frame filled the space.

"Juniper, get your head out of that book," he said. "Let's go and practice your free throws."

Rose slipped under his arm, giving Juniper a sympathetic look backward. Juniper's shoulders tensed. Her stomach began to hurt.

Their dad was the tallest person Juniper had ever seen in person. He was the reason she was currently on track to be recruited into the circus. *Step right up and see the tallest girl in the world!*

He bent over her desk to peer at the book she had open. He picked it up and flipped it to read the cover. "Physics?" he said "You reading this just for fun?"

"I checked it out from the library," Juniper said.

She felt weirdly embarrassed and placed her hand over the cover as if to hide a secret. When she'd seen the book sitting in the science section, it was like she couldn't help but take it home. She'd wanted to know all of the secrets in those pages.

"How'd you get into physics? Rose was never into physics," her dad said. He shook his head as if he didn't understand. Rose had received a full-ride college scholarship for basketball, of course. She was thinking of studying to be a teacher, though.

"Let's go shoot some hoops, Junebug," he boomed. He grabbed the physics book and threw it onto the bed like it was nothing.

Juniper didn't want to practice her free throws. The humiliation of the previous game washed over her. Veronica's nasty words—*double choke*—went through her mind. But she stood, grabbed a sweatshirt, and began to pull on her high tops.

She remembered Rose telling her that she was tough. She wasn't so sure.

Her dad walked out, whistling. At least he wasn't frustrated with her anymore.

Juniper thumped down the stairs in huge shoes that could have belonged to clown. Her mother, a music teacher, was in the living room playing the piano. With her black hair pulled up into a bun and her face free from make-up, her mom looked like a teenager. She was beautiful.

At twelve, Juniper already towered over her mother. Why did she have to get the super-tall gene?

Juniper sat down on the bench next to her mom. She began to play the lower notes. The harmony of the music between them came to life. Juniper's heart seemed to beat with the rhythm of the notes as she played the piano keys. She and her mother's long fingers moved together over the keyboard, fast and lively.

Juniper had taken lessons from her mom ever since she'd been able to reach the keys. She'd loved every minute of it.

The music shifted with the crescendo and leaped out of the piano. When they came to the end of the song, they smiled at each other. Juniper felt the softness of her mom ease something inside of her.

"You're my favorite piano partner," her mom said.

At the piano, Juniper suddenly realized that, sitting down, she and her mother were the same height. A normal height.

She thought about that. Maybe it was the main reason she loved playing the piano so much. On the court, Juniper always stood out with her long giraffe legs and bony elbows and knees.

Too soon, her dad was standing behind her. "C'mon kid," he said. "Lets go shoot."

He looked so earnest and excited that Juniper instantly stood up and followed him out to the driveway. He'd lined up drills for her to do. She did them with as much enthusiasm as she could muster.

Shuffle, turn, catch, shoot. Shuffle, turn, catch, shoot. Shuffle, turn, catch, shoot . . .

Over and over they practiced the drills until sweat dripped off of Juniper's nose. She bent over and grabbed her knees, her legs shaking. She told herself that all of the practice would make a difference. She told herself that she was steadily improving.

"You're really working hard out here, Junebug," her dad said. He patted her on the back.

"You're so lucky to be as tall as you are." He passed her the ball, and it slapped into her wide palms. "I was so short when I was your age. That's why Uncle Matt still calls me Pee-Wee."

They both laughed at this. Juniper's dad was definitely not a pee-wee.

Juniper took a jump shot. The ball swished in.

She felt a mixture of feelings. There was a lightness from his compliment. There was also a heavy feeling of sadness for her dad.

She'd knew that he hadn't been able to play much basketball when he was young. He'd been short until almost college, and by then it was too late. She knew he put a lot of pressure on her because she was lucky to be tall when it mattered.

Underneath all of these feelings, equations and numbers floated through her mind like the notes on the piano. They made sense to her in an ordered, logical way. They were simple. To Juniper, basketball was chaos—no matter how hard she practiced, she felt she could never predict exactly what was going to happen in a game.

Juniper placed her hands precisely on the ball. It was the exact hand placement her dad had shown her many times to shoot straight and true.

She imagined herself all alone under the hoop.

Mila had just passed her the ball. She had lined her body up to put the ball into the basket.

She lifted her right arm up and shot the ball. It flew through the air, banked off the backboard, and swished through the net. It made that lovely whisper of a sound.

"Nice shot, Juney!" her dad shouted.

The pride in his voice made her feel like she could accomplish anything.

There was no crowd though.

It was just Juniper and her dad in the driveway. Juniper was afraid that Veronica was right. She was a choker. And in a real game, probably, she would likely just choke again.

Juniper didn't want to admit to herself that the beautiful shot still felt forced. It felt, somehow, like work.

She thought about basketball and wondered if she'd ever feel at ease playing the game.

Basketball had never come natural to her, Juniper began to realize. Not like it seemed to for her dad or her sister. Not like the beautiful symmetry of the equations that were floating through her mind. Not like the musical notes that sang to her. The notes that told her to go back inside to the piano and play and play and play.

CHAPTER 3

ZONE DEFENSE

Juniper laced up her bright white high tops.

The girls on her junior varsity team chattered happily in the locker room. Their energies were high because it was game day. They slapped high fives and made stupid jokes about the boys in their class.

Only Juniper was silent and worried. She'd practiced. She'd done the drills. She'd memorized the plays. But she just couldn't shake the feeling that she hadn't done enough. That whatever she needed to be, she wouldn't be it.

"Try not to choke today, Jackson," Veronica said. She threw a dirty towel at Juniper that landed on her shoes with a wet plop. "We all know you're only starting because your dad's the coach."

A couple of the other girls snickered. They weren't quite brave enough to laugh out loud.

Juniper turned toward her locker and ignored Veronica. Her parents had taught her to ignore anyone that was being a bully. Still, Juniper had to bite her tongue hard.

Mila's high voice cut through the room. "Shut up, Veronica," she said. She stood with her hands on her hips right in front of Veronica. She looked like a ferocious elf. "Juniper's already a better player than you'll ever be."

Veronica raised her eyebrows. "We'll see about that," she said.

Juniper thought it was nice of Mila to stick up for her. Mila probably didn't realize that Juniper thought

Veronica was probably right. Veronica wasn't the only one who believed that Juniper started because of her dad. Juniper actually believed it herself.

Veronica probably deserved to start in Juniper's place. Juniper had potential. But at this point, Veronica was more aggressive.

Juniper wanted to prove herself. She wanted to show everyone that she wasn't just starting at center because of her dad. Or because she was the tallest girl on the team. She wanted to prove that she deserved to start.

After warm-ups, the buzzer sounded. It was time to play the game.

On the opening jump ball, Juniper easily tipped the ball to the Panthers forward, Sarah. Sometimes being a giraffe was helpful.

Sarah passed to Mila, who dribbled down the left wing to set up their offensive play. Juniper set herself up in the low post area.

Sarah was about to come and screen Juniper's defender so that she could get an open shot near the free throw line. The buzz from the crowd gave Juniper a needed boost of energy.

Sarah screened for Juniper, who moved swiftly on her long legs. Mila passed Juniper the ball. Juniper caught it, squared up, and shot. She felt that rare magic of movement in every part of her.

Swish.

The Panthers were two points up.

"Great shot, Juniper!" her dad shouted.

Juniper could feel warmth spread through her. There was no better feeling in the world than making her dad proud.

"Hustle back, now," Juniper's dad said. "Hustle back and play some defense!"

The first and second quarters went by in blur. Juniper made two more shots and blocked three. After one of her nice plays, she also managed to smirk toward the bench at Veronica as she ran down the court. Juniper knew it wasn't a mature thing to do, but she couldn't help it.

The opponents, the Spartans, were tough. Only two points separated the teams when the buzzer for halftime went off. Juniper had only come out of the game once for a rest. Her legs were wobbly with exhaustion. Her heart, though, was light.

In the locker room, Juniper's dad stood in front of the team. "Great job out there, girls," he said. "But they're still killing us under the basket." He drew some X's and O's on the board to show the girls how to improve their play.

"Juniper," he said, "I really need you to step it up out there on defense. Their center is tossing them in left and right. Maybe we'll try a zone defense."

"Oh no," someone said off to Juniper's right.

Juniper looked up sharply. The Panthers had not practiced their zone defense very much. This would be a new challenge for everyone. Juniper felt guilty about that.

It was her fault they had to change the defense. She'd been too slow. This had given the Spartans some easy points. She knew her dad was right to single her out but still wished he wouldn't.

He continued to draw diagrams to demonstrate the defensive change. He put an exclamation point by the circle that represented Juniper. "Use those long arms!" he shouted.

Veronica and a couple of her minions chuckled. Someone whispered, "Sasquatch arms, he means."

Juniper could feel the anger spread through her like a hot coals. She couldn't help that she was tall. Plus, she *had* been working hard out there.

Her dad could have talked about how great Mila was passing. Or, how Sarah had stolen the ball three times. But his focus was on her, and this made her feel bad for the other players.

They all put their hands together and shouted, "Go Panthers!"

Juniper felt hot and angry. She couldn't let go of her frustration.

The buzzer sounded. The starters jogged out onto the court to begin the second half.

The Spartans threw the ball in.

Juniper's body was filled with bottled-up anger. She set herself up under the basket, trying to remember the defensive plan and what she was supposed to do. She didn't know where to stand. Her mind whirled with black X's and O's.

She began to think about the halftime speech. It was like when he looked at her, he saw only disappointment. In her anger, she completely forgot that he'd been giving her some good advice, too.

The Spartans point guard drove to the hoop. In an instant, she scooped the ball up into the basket before Juniper could help out and go for the block.

Juniper hadn't been paying attention to the game. Now the two teams were tied up.

Juniper rushed down the court to sounds of her dad yelling. "Come on, Juniper," he said. "Play hard!"

After that, the game felt like total chaos to Juniper. The Spartans racked up six more points in just a couple of minutes. Juniper felt like she was running in mud. She felt like she was always two seconds behind the play. As she slogged down the court after she'd failed to block out yet *another* rebound, she heard her dad shouting for a timeout.

The ref blew his whistle.

In the huddle, Juniper's dad got right in her face. "What's going on out there, Juniper?" he said. He sounded furious.

Juniper could feel the rest of the team's eyes go wide.

"I . . . I don't know," Juniper said. She realized she was nearly crying.

"That's not good enough," he said. "Go sit at the end of the bench." He pointed his finger at Veronica. "Get in there, Veronica," he said. "Show Juniper how to be aggressive."

Juniper felt humiliated.

CHAPTER 4

BENCHED

Veronica ran out onto the court. The back of her navy jersey flashing the number twenty-five. Veronica looked like she was focused. She looked like she was ready to take charge. The crowd cheered at the change in players. Juniper felt claws of jealousy pierce her skin.

Veronica grabbed a rebound in the first possession, blocking out two Spartans. She tossed the ball to Mila, who dashed down the court. The claws dug deeper.

Mila swerved in and out. She cut between three defending Spartans like a dart. When she got to the basket, she flicked the ball up. Her lay-up glided through the net like a dream.

Juniper cheered for her friend and felt proud of her. But she also couldn't help but think that she'd been the source of her team's unlucky streak.

"Turn it around!" Juniper's dad shouted. "Get back on defense!" He wasn't thinking about Juniper now. He was into the game.

Juniper pulled at the edges of her shorts and tried to look as tiny as possible. The other girls ignored her. It was like they were worried that her terrible playing might be contagious.

Mila chased down the Spartans guard. She got in front of her and forced her to pass. A Spartan guard took a shot from the three-point line.

The ball circled the rim and fell out. Veronica had a good position and jumped high for the rebound.

Juniper knew she needed to be more aggressive like Veronica. She wasn't entirely comfortable throwing around her new tall body. Sometimes when she moved, it was like she was trying to control something that didn't even belong to her.

The Panthers took over on offense. Veronica set a pick for Mila and rolled to the basket. Mila hit Veronica with a perfect pass, and Veronica finished off the play with a short bucket.

The Panthers kept going and reeled off ten points in a row. The hot streak seemed to Juniper to have everything to do with Veronica being in the game. And Juniper being on the bench. After another five minutes, the game—mercifully for Juniper— was over.

The buzzer sounded, and the Panthers erupted from the bench, jumping up and down. They had won. They all gathered around Veronica and hugged her and clapped her on the back. Veronica was the hero.

Juniper watched. She felt like she didn't deserve to be a part of the celebration. She watched her dad give Veronica a high five.

Juniper felt tears pricking her eyes. She left the bench and darted off to the locker room without shaking the hands of the Spartans. She was being a bad sport, she knew. She would get into trouble.

She didn't care.

Moments later, the Panthers came into the locker room. Juniper felt her teammates go quiet when they saw her. She couldn't even look at them.

Juniper's dad stormed into the locker room behind the team. He walked directly over to Juniper. When Juniper looked up, she saw thunderclouds in his eyes.

He pointed a finger at Juniper. "If I ever see another disrespectful display like that, Juniper Jackson, you won't lace up those high-tops on my court ever again."

Silence fell like a curtain.

The other players stared at their fidgeting fingers. Juniper turned white-hot with embarrassment. She'd known that she'd been wrong, but she couldn't believe that he was humiliating her in front of the entire team. Again.

Before she could help it, Juniper felt her mouth foolishly opening. "Well, maybe I don't even want to be on this team," she said.

She regretted the words the instantly.

A long, agonizing pause followed. Juniper wished the floor would swallow her up.

"That's fine," said her dad. He threaded his fingers together. And then in a voice that was soft and almost too calm, he said, "You're off the team."

He turned and stalked out of the locker room, leaving a deadly silence in his wake.

Juniper didn't know what to do. She'd made a terrible mess of things.

In the minutes that followed, uneasiness cloaked the air around Juniper. She felt utterly alone and wanted to chase after her dad and apologize, but her pride stopped her.

No one looked at her, talked to her, or even came near her. Even Veronica ignored her, like she wasn't worth picking on anymore.

Juniper gathered her things slowly, deliberately, not meeting anyone's eyes. She couldn't believe she'd said she didn't want to be on the team. *What had she been thinking?*

"Hey, June," Mila's small voice said, interrupting her misery. "You want a ride home?" Her friend peered up at her with worry in her eyes. Mila had correctly assumed that Juniper didn't want to ride home with her dad.

Juniper nodded, not trusting herself to speak. The tears were too close to the surface. One word and they might start to fall.

Juniper gathered up her things and packed them away as quickly as she could. She walked out of the locker room alongside Mila, not knowing what she would face.

CHAPTER 5

OUT OF THE GAME

The morning after the game, Juniper slunk downstairs. She was starving. Otherwise she would have hidden in her room all day.

The night before, Juniper's dad had acted as if she didn't exist. Now, he sat at the head of the table. He scrolled through the news on his phone and didn't look up when she entered.

Juniper's mom bustled around the kitchen. Delicious smells came from everywhere.

"Good morning, Juniper," her mom said.

Juniper's stomach grumbled, and she pressed a hand to it, as if to shush it.

"Good morning to your stomach too, I guess?" her mom asked, grinning at her.

Juniper managed a weak smile in return.

Her mom placed a huge plate of pancakes in front of Juniper. They were golden brown with steam rising from them.

Pancakes were Juniper's favorite. And her dad's favorite. It was obvious that her mom was trying to create some kind of peace between them.

"I made bacon, too," her mom said. She opened the oven to pull out a platter of more wonderful-smelling food.

Juniper's mouth watered. She started to pile pancakes onto her plate and drench them with syrup.

She could see her dad peeking up from his phone and then reaching for a plate. He was interested in breakfast, at least.

After a few bites, the sugar pulsing through her veins, Juniper had a surge of bravery. She needed to let her dad know that she knew she'd been wrong. She needed to let him know that she was sorry. She *did* want to be a part of his team.

"Dad?" she started, scared but determined.

"Hmm?" he said, not moving his eyes away from his phone. He put another forkful of pancake into his mouth.

"I'm really sorry about last night," Juniper said. "I should have been a better sport and, um, I *do* want to be on your team."

He didn't say anything.

Juniper added, "If you'll let me, that is."

He looked her in the eyes then, taking her measure to see if she was serious. His eyes softened, "Thank you for saying sorry," he said. "That shows real maturity. I *am* really disappointed, however, in your actions."

She stared down into the pile of pancakes and bacon and syrup. It was all getting cold. Her appetite was suddenly gone.

"But . . . ," he said. Juniper looked up at the word, hope blooming in her. "I know you've been practicing hard this past week. You'll miss the game tomorrow night, and then let's talk more."

"Okay," she said. She decided her punishment for being disrespectful was fair. "I'll practice all day today. And tomorrow. You'll see, dad."

"I guess I will," he said.

When the sides of his eyes crinkled, Juniper knew she was mostly forgiven. With that, he got up and put his plate in the dishwasher and left the kitchen.

"Hey, honey," her mom said, sitting down in the chair next to her. "You got this flyer in the mail today."

She slid a piece of paper toward Juniper. On the top it said, *Science and Physics Camp! Come and learn how the world works!*

"Oh, cool," Juniper said. "I've been waiting for this." Juniper felt a little thrill of excitement. Her dad was going to let her back on the team, *and* she was going to get to go to science camp.

Juniper's mom gave her a worried look.

"What is it?" asked Juniper.

"Well," said her mom, "it's just that the date of the science camp is unfortunate. It's the same date as your dad's basketball camp."

Oh no, Juniper thought. *What am I going to do?*

Juniper always helped her dad with his basketball camp. She coached the younger kids, teaching them plays and drills and games. It was one of her favorite weekends out of the year.

But she'd also really been looking forward to the science camp—for a long time. If she chose the science camp, how could she ever tell her dad? She'd only just been forgiven. Juniper felt like her world was torn in half. She wished that she didn't have to make such tough decisions.

* * *

Juniper spent the next week trying to prove
herself. She got up early each morning. She practiced
out in the driveway for an hour before school. She
shot extra free throws each night—long after the
other girls had gone home. She hoped it was enough.

One night, she rounded the top of the three-point
line, tossing up one ball after another. She thought
about how she didn't know if her dad had ever really
seen her. The real her.

The next night, Juniper sat at the end of the
bench. She dressed in her street clothes for the game.
She endured her punishment. Most of her teammates
had been kind to her after her dad explained her
one-game suspension. He'd reminded them about the
importance of being respectful. He said that being a
good sport was really the *only* thing he cared about.

He'd patted her shoulder then and added, "I'm
really proud of Juniper for saying sorry, however."

Juniper had seen Veronica whispering with Sarah. Both girls hid their mouths with their hands like they were laughing at her. She wished that they would be called out for being disrespectful for once.

The Panthers played a tough game, coming out with a two-point win.

As Juniper had watched from the end of the bench, she felt some jealousy. Mostly, she just wanted to get out there and play. She missed the feeling of the ball in her hands or throwing the perfect pass. She missed the powerful feeling of being able to reach her long arms above the other players. To tip a jump ball or toss in a lay-up. She missed grabbing a rebound. She missed bringing the ball down into her chest, feeling like it belonged to her.

All of those feelings surprised her.

On the drive home from the game, her dad talked cheerfully about the team. "I think that the girls really stepped up and played together. That was a good team victory."

Juniper joined in. "I thought Mila really shined. She was the high-scorer." Just talking about the game together made their relationship feel normal again.

"Next game," he said, "you won't be starting. I'm proud of all the extra practice you've put in. But you'll need to prove yourself again."

Despite the demotion, Juniper felt hope flutter in her chest like a hummingbird. She *had* practiced every spare moment since she'd been benched. She was glad that he'd noticed. She wanted to show him she could do it.

Now was the moment to let him know about the camp. She'd made her decision and knew that he wouldn't be happy about it. She hoped that the Panthers win had put him in more of an understanding mood.

"So, uh, Dad?" Juniper said. She stared out the window at the passing trees. "There's this science camp coming up that I'd really like to go to."

"Sure thing, June. It's great that you love science." He smiled at her in the rearview mirror.

"Well . . . ," she said. Her palms began to sweat. "The thing is, it's the same weekend as your basketball camp." She looked up to see his reaction.

He frowned deeply. He gripped and un-gripped the steering wheel. Juniper's heart sank. He was mad.

After an agonizing moment, he said, "No, that's fine. You do what you need to do."

They turned into their driveway. He slowed to a stop. He pulled the keys from the ignition a little harder than necessary. "I just wish," he said, "you'd choose basketball, for once."

Juniper sat in the driveway all by herself.

The basketball hoop stared down at her like an accusation.

CHAPTER 6

SIMPLE SCIENCE

Juniper was at science camp, in an introductory physics class. New friends surrounded her. These kids seemed to share her love for science.

The teacher stood in front of the room. She had written on the board: *The Theory of Motion.*

"Would anybody like to come up to the front of the room and put this theory into practice?" she asked. "A volunteer, please?"

Juniper raised her hand. The teacher spotted her right away. Juniper's arm was, after all, much longer than everybody else's.

"The young lady with the black hair and the navy Panthers sweatshirt," said the teacher. "Come on down."

Juniper was elated. As she jogged down the stairs, she thought to herself, *Sometimes being tall does have its advantages.*

The teacher reached behind her desk and pulled out a small basketball. Juniper was confused.

The teacher handed the ball to Juniper. "All right now, she said. "Please shoot the basketball into the basket."

"Shoot it?" Juniper said. "Where?"

The teacher pointed toward the door. Sure enough, there was a mini basketball hoop fitted over the top of the door. Juniper didn't know how she'd missed it.

"From this line to the door is the exact distance of a free throw," the teacher said. "Fifteen feet."

Juniper smiled. She lined her body up with hoop. She did it exactly how she would normally shoot. She flexed her arm up and tossed the ball in an arc. The ball clattered against the rim and bounced out.

Juniper shrugged. The class laughed.

The teacher retrieved the ball. "Get into your shooting position again," she said. "This time I'm going to place your arm a little differently." She handed the ball to Juniper.

Juniper let the teacher adjust her arm, moving the elbow up about six inches.

"Try shooting at this angle," said the teacher.

Juniper went through the motion a few times. The angle felt strange to her. The fourth time, Juniper let the ball go. It curved high and then dropped. Juniper heard the *swish* of the ball falling through the net. A perfect shot.

The room erupted into cheers.

Juniper turned to the teacher in amazement.

"You see?" the teacher said, "Many things in our world come down to simple physics. When you shoot a free throw, your launch angle should be around forty-five degrees."

Juniper thought about that. It made sense.

"At first, you were shooting at around forty degrees, which is too low," the teacher said. "It's simple science. And by the way, you're lucky to be so very tall."

Juniper looked down at the teacher, who was about five feet tall.

The teacher looked over the rim of her glasses at Juniper. "You'll command a lot of attention when you're a scientist."

Juniper blushed. The comment actually pleased her, though.

The teacher dismissed Juniper back to her seat. She began to discuss the physics surrounding the theory of motion. The teacher's words floated through the air.

Juniper's mind drifted. She had the strangest realization start to bubble up inside. *It was all just simple science.* The teacher continued to talk. Juniper sat in stunned silence.

Her new friend, Caleb, turned and stared at her. "What's wrong?" Caleb asked. Concern pulled down his thick eyebrows behind his glasses.

"It's all just science!" Juniper whispered to him. Her mind churned through a million thoughts. Numbers and words clicked into place like a giant jigsaw puzzle.

"Yeah?" Caleb said, looking at her like that was the most obvious thing ever.

"Basketball," said Juniper, "is just . . . physics."

Juniper was floored.

She'd never thought about it before. But she could apply all of the physics theories she'd been learning about to basketball.

Motion theories applied to dribbling.

Energy theories applied to rebounding.

Rotation theories applied to passing.

Angle theories applied to shooting.

Caleb stared at Juniper like she'd just grown two heads. Juniper didn't care. Basketball made a new sort of sense to her suddenly, and Juniper couldn't wait to talk to her dad about it.

Her dad.

Thinking about him made the volcano of guilt she felt for missing his basketball camp boil up. She hoped he'd forgive her.

CHAPTER 7

BASKETBALL CAMP

Juniper watched her teammates playing basketball with the younger kids. Her heart sunk. It looked like everyone had made it to the basketball camp. Everyone except for her.

She recognized some of the little kids from the year before. Chloe, a first grader, was getting lessons on how to steal the ball from Mila. Chloe ran up behind Mila and popped the ball forward while the older girl dribbled. Chloe looked up at Mila with hero worship shining in her eyes.

There was Nadine, a taller, serious third grader. She reminded Juniper of herself at that age. She and Sarah were working on rebounding. Nadine was listening to Sarah as if the older girl knew all of the secrets to basketball.

Veronica was working with a group of kids on proper shooting form. She helped a boy push his elbow straight and bend his wrist at the end. She gave him a high five when he got it right. Juniper was amazed that Veronica was being so cool.

Juniper spied her dad laughing with Nadine. She overheard her dad say, "The most important thing is that you had fun."

Nadine beamed. She ran off to greet her mother. Juniper remembered the time when her dad used to say that same thing to her. Juniper had forgotten that. They used to have fun while playing basketball. These days, he was all about being perfect.

And winning.

She wished that she could help him remember the fun.

"Got ya!"

Juniper was pummeled from behind by a duo of giggling bodies. She had to step forward to keep her balance. Howls of laughter surrounded her. It was Henry and Liam, the twins with the orange curls. Last year, she'd taught them how to dribble between their legs. That's all they'd practiced the rest of the camp.

"Hey, you little twerps," Juniper said, hugging them. "How's camp been this year?"

"We missed you!" Henry yelled.

Juniper grinned. "I missed you, too," she said.

Just then, Juniper's dad blew his whistle. "Find your team!" he yelled.

Running away, the boys fell over each other like puppies. The campers grouped into separate sides. They pushed and shoved and laughed.

The enthusiasm was catching. Juniper felt like she'd really missed out on something. But then she remembered her flash of insight at science camp. She smiled to herself. It was like she had an amazing secret inside of her.

"Juniper!" Mila shouted when she spotted her tall teammate.

"Hey, Mila," said Juniper.

"I'm coaching the Green Goblins," Mila said.

"Grrr!" a little boy with black hair growled and curled his fingers into claws. "We're gonna eat that other team up!"

"Help me, will you please?" Mila said looking worried. She was trying to help Nadine with her jersey. Nadine's head how somehow ended up in an armhole.

"Sure," said Juniper, laughing. She picked up more green jerseys and tossed them to the remaining members of the Green Goblin team.

The game was wild but fun. Mostly, the seventh-grade coaches tried to keep the littler kids from traveling. Or running out of bounds. Or shooting at the wrong basket.

Once, while taking the ball down the court, Henry managed to dribble the ball between his legs. "Did you see that?" he shouted at Juniper.

As he waited for Juniper's response, another camper snuck up. He stole the ball and took off.

Juniper laughed out loud. "I saw it!" she shouted.

The Green Goblins played hard against the Lightning Bolts. The kids were hustling, laughing, and sweating.

During a timeout, Mila coached the kids. After the timeout, Nadine would have two free throws coming up. Mila reminded the rest to be ready for the rebound in case Nadine missed.

"Mind if I say something?" Juniper asked Mila.

"Shoot," said Mila.

Juniper joined the huddle. "Okay, Nadine," she said. "So, when you shoot the ball, I want you to put your elbow at this angle." She adjusted Nadine's elbow. "And when you release the ball, it should travel in a nice high arc of about forty-five degrees."

"What's forty-five degrees?" Nadine asked.

"Like this," Juniper said. She drew an imaginary curved line in the air. "If you shoot with too low of an arc, the ball doesn't have the best chance to go in. If you shoot at a forty-five-degree angle, it'll work better. It's *scientifically proven* to work."

Nadine nodded at Juniper, her gaze serious.

The Green Goblins ran back out onto the court. Nadine walked to the free throw line. She flexed her arm over and over, practicing getting the right imaginary arc.

While Nadine stood there, all of the other campers were quiet for once. It was as if they knew something magical was going to happen.

Nadine bounced the ball once, then twice.

She lifted the ball up to her shoulder height. She threw the ball up at what looked like something close to forty-five degrees. The ball flew in a beautiful, bending rainbow. It came down and swished through the net.

The kids all cheered. Even the Lightning Bolts.

Nadine smiled shyly at Juniper.

Soon the game was over. Time was up. The campers scurried to their parents. Juniper spied her dad standing alone. She walked over to him.

"Hey Dad," Juniper said. "Looks like it turned out to be a great camp." She felt sheepish saying it.

He looked up from his clipboard and gave her a smile. She hadn't been expecting that.

"Hey there, Junebug," he said. He put a long arm around her.

"This was a lot of *fun*, Dad," Juniper said. She emphasized the word, *fun* hoping he would realize she'd heard him talking to Nadine.

"You're right," he said.

They both watched as all of the little kids ran and laughed and tackled each other.

"*We* used to have fun," Juniper said sadly.

He dad looked at her for a long moment. He seemed confused. "We always have fun playing basketball, don't we Junebug?"

She frowned.

He gave her shoulder a squeeze and turned away to talk to some parents.

Juniper felt badly as she watched him chat with Henry and Liam's mom. He still didn't understand.

CHAPTER 8

SISTERLY ADVICE

The next Friday night, Juniper's sister, Rose, came home from college again. Her entire family was excited to see her. They couldn't wait to hear all about her adventures at school. As they ate dinner, Rose told stories about her college basketball team.

Rose scooped piles of mashed potatoes on her plate as she talked. "So, every player on the team was the best player from her own hometown," she said. "One day, we decided to have a contest to see who could make the most three-pointers in a row."

Juniper watched Rose grab another chicken leg and pile more broccoli on her plate. Rose had told them earlier that the dorm food was terrible.

"So, we all took a turn," she continued. "Shot after shot, until there was only me and two other girls left who hadn't missed. We were at five in a row each."

The entire Jackson family leaned forward. They were eager to hear how her story would end.

"I shot first," Rose said, taking a huge bite of peas. "Swish. It went in as smooth as butter."

Juniper's dad beamed, "That's my girl. It's all that extra practice I made you do."

Rose rolled her eyes at her dad.

Juniper laughed.

"Sure, Dad," Rose said. "You are the best coach and father, yada, yada."

He chuckled at Rose poking fun. He seemed more relaxed when Rose was around.

"Anyway, I made my shot," Rose continued. "Then the next girl went. The ball hit the rim and bounced out."

"Then came Jasmine. She is *not* friendly," said Rose. "She's one of those girls who can't ever be happy for someone else." Rose looked over at Juniper and asked, "You know that type of girl?"

"Do I ever," Juniper said. She looked down at her plate, thinking of Veronica and her minions.

"So Jasmine lines up her arm and is about to let go," Rose said, pausing for effect. "And just at that moment, a huge poster fell from the side of the gym! It clattered to the ground right beside us. We all jumped and screamed."

Juniper watched Rose tear off another hunk of chicken with her teeth.

"Jasmine was startled, and the ball went wonky in the air," Rose said, her mouth full of food. "It was like even the *universe* didn't want her to win."

The entire family laughed.

"Well, that wasn't the weirdest thing," Rose said. "The weirdest thing was that I actually felt bad about laughing at Jasmine."

Juniper stopped mid-bite. Now *she* felt bad for laughing.

"So I let her shoot again," Rose said, looking specifically at Juniper.

"What happened?" Juniper asked.

"She won," Rose said simply, chewing. "She made two more in a row. I only made one. But then she congratulated me and, actually, she's one of my closest friends now. Girls are strange."

"That's great, honey," her mother said. She looked proudly at her oldest daughter.

Juniper was amazed. She thought about what it might be like to try to be nice to Veronica. It would be hard.

Juniper gazed around at her family.

Her dad was laughing at something Rose had said. Her mom grinned at the both of them. Juniper loved it when her family was together like that. She wished Rose still lived at home.

After the girls cleaned up the dishes, Rose snapped a wet towel at Juniper's leg. She barely missed. "Wanna go shoot some hoops little sister?" Rose asked.

"Sure," Juniper said. "But I'm taller than you. So, really, who's the *little* sister?"

* * *

Juniper passed Rose the basketball. It was twilight, and the sun had slid behind a cloud. The sky was a mixture of pink and purple streaks. A mourning dove cooed. The world felt peaceful to Juniper.

Except that she was losing at H-O-R-S-E.

Juniper had an R. Rose had only an H.

Juniper sunk one in from all the way across the driveway.

"Nice shot, *little* sister," Rose taunted and bounced the ball on the asphalt. "You've improved these last few months."

Juniper scowled. "Tell Dad that," she said.

"Uh-oh. Is he still getting on you a lot?" Rose asked. She lined up where Juniper had made her shot. She aimed and let go. The ball arced through the air, circled the rim, and finally went in. "Yes!" Rose shouted. She pumped her fist.

"Lucky shot," said Juniper. "And yeah, you could say dad is getting on me a lot," Juniper said.

"Oh man," Rose said. "Seventh grade was the toughest year," She dribbled behind her back and then passed the ball to Juniper. "He was so nice to everyone else and so hard on me."

Facing away from the rim, Juniper threw the ball into a backward arc toward the basket.

The ball bounced out.

"It's like I can barely ever do anything right for him," Juniper said. "And he puts so much pressure on me because I'm tall. Or because I'm his daughter, I suppose."

It was Rose's turn. She lobbed up a perfect hook shot through the air. It swished in like magic.

Juniper groaned. That was going to be a hard one to replicate.

Rose said, "You know he was a short kid, right?" She passed to Juniper.

"Yeah, I knew that," Juniper said. She caught the flying ball as it whizzed toward her.

"But did you know that in seventh grade," Rose said, "he was a benchwarmer? It wasn't like it is now, where everybody gets in. He spent a whole season on the bench."

"Really?" Juniper said. She paused to look at her sister.

"Can you imagine?" Rose said. "Sitting on the bench all year? Working your tail off in practice and never once getting to go into the game?"

"He did tell me he almost quit playing after that year," Juniper said.

"Yeah," Rose said. "I thought about that a lot when he was being extra bossy." She grinned up at her little sister.

Their shadows spread out beneath them on the sidewalk. Juniper's shadow was lean and long and inches taller than Rose's.

"You've grown a lot this year, " Rose said. "You've got to be, what, eight feet tall by now?"

"Probably," Juniper said. "Look, even my shadow is as skinny and tall as a flagpole."

"I grew a lot in seventh grade, too," Rose said. "It was awesome."

"Awesome?" Juniper said. "You mean that you actually liked being tall when you were younger? For real?"

"Of course! Back then, even the boys wanted me on their basketball team. I was *way* taller than any of them."

Juniper thought about her sister playing on a seventh grade boys team and laughed. She then thought about how she was wasting her height by being ashamed of it. She thought about what the science teacher saying about her being able to command attention. Her height made her different. But maybe different could come in handy.

Juniper threw the hook shot over her head to try and match Rose's shot.

Swish!

"Woo-hoo!" Juniper shouted.

Rose gave her a high five. They continued to play their game, giggling and teasing each other. Juniper thought about how much fun it was when she didn't think about *having* to be the best. She wondered if it had been her dad making her feel that pressure. Or maybe she'd been doing it to herself all along.

Rose missed an easy layup and fell to the ground in mock agony. Juniper cracked up until she had to clutch her sides in pain. The sisters howled and rolled until tears came to their eyes. The neighbor dogs started barking at the ruckus.

When they recovered, they got up and put in shot after shot. Juniper thought all the while about physics theories and angles. About rotation theories and the wonderful symmetry of it all. She ended up losing to her sister by one letter. She didn't care, though.

For the first time in a while, basketball felt beautiful. It was like a symphony, with all the instruments lined up. The ball. Her giraffe legs. The basket. Her sister's flawlessly arced shots. It was perfect in its own unruly way.

Juniper couldn't remember the last time she'd had that much fun playing basketball. Neither girl noticed their dad watching them closely from an open window.

Neither girl noticed the gloomy look on his face.

Later that night, Juniper got up to get a glass of water. She overheard Rose and her dad talking in the living room. Juniper crept closer and stayed as quiet as possible.

"I think you've got to take it a little easier on her," Rose said.

"What do you mean?" their dad said.

"I mean, it's really hard being *your* kid on *your* team," said Rose.

Juniper could feel her heart hammering in her chest. She couldn't believe Rose was confronting him. She also didn't want to get caught eavesdropping.

"Was I really too hard on you?" their dad said.

"Let's just say I was glad you were only my coach for one year," Rose said.

There was a long pause.

"She did say something strange to me the other day," he said finally. "She said we *used* to have fun playing basketball."

"Basketball has got to be fun at least some of the time," Rose said. "Right?"

I was watching you two out in the driveway tonight," their dad said. "I haven't seen Junebug look that happy playing ball in awhile."

Juniper had heard enough. She tiptoed back up the stairs as quietly as she could on her big feet.

CHAPTER 9

GAME DAY

Juniper sat and warmed the end of the bench again. She had been demoted to the second string, and Veronica was going to start in her place. Despite all of this, she was excited.

Before the game, Juniper had pulled Veronica aside. "I know you'll do great out there," she said. She patted Veronica on the back.

Veronica smiled awkwardly. "Uh . . . thanks?" she'd said. She seemed perplexed that Juniper was being kind to her.

Juniper didn't know why herself. She just didn't want any more bad feelings while playing basketball. She'd found the fun in the game again, and she wanted to keep it. She hoped her dad felt the same.

The starters took their places on the court for the opening tipoff.

"Go Panthers!" Juniper shouted.

The rest of the team clapped and cheered. Her dad looked down at her and actually grinned. Juniper felt hope bloom in her belly.

The Panthers were playing the best team in their district, the Warriors. They had lost to them by only one point earlier in the season.

The navy jerseys of the Panthers were in sharp contrast to the bright green uniforms of the Warriors. The girls on both teams looked pumped and ready to play.

Juniper was surprised to see that one of the Warriors players looked nearly as tall as she was.

Had she grown since they played last? Maybe. But number fifteen didn't look uncomfortable with her new height. She looked proud and sure. That's probably how Rose had looked in seventh grade. Juniper wanted to be like that.

The whistle blew. Veronica leaped high into the air for the tip-off. She managed to swat the ball to Sarah. Sarah threw the ball to Mila. The Panthers lined up their offensive play.

The Warriors spread out into a zone defense.

"Pass it!" Juniper's dad shouted.

The Panthers passed the basketball around the court. Once, twice. On the third pass, number fifteen from the Warriors reached out her long arm. She deflected the ball. It bounced toward the Warriors point guard.

Juniper held her breath.

The Warriors point guard snagged the ball and was off like a shot down the court.

She rocketed a pass toward one of the forwards. The forward launched a shot from the three-point line. In it went.

The crowd cheered.

The Warriors were off to a good start.

Mila took the ball down, dribbling expertly. She darted past one defender and then two. She got stuck at the top of the key, Warriors surrounding her. In a desperate move, she tossed the ball away blindly.

The ball floated for a through the air. Veronica dashed forward. She snatched the ball from right beneath the basket and swung it up into the air. But as the ball went into the hoop, her body dropped suddenly. Veronica lay slumped on the ground. She rocked, holding her ankle.

The ref blew his whistle to stop play.

Oh no, Juniper thought. *She's hurt.*

The Panthers team trainer and Juniper's dad ran out onto the court. They knelt beside Veronica. The whole gymnasium went quiet.

After a moment, the trainer helped Veronica stand up. The crowd clapped in support. Veronica limped off the court with the trainer holding her up.

As they passed Juniper, Veronica stared her directly in the eye. "Try not to screw up my game, okay, Jackson?" she said to Juniper.

Juniper saw that Veronica's ankle was already beginning to swell up. Veronica wouldn't likely be coming back to play against the Warriors.

"I think I can manage," Juniper said.

And then the most amazing thing happened: Veronica laughed out loud. She extended her fist. Juniper bumped it. She had the strangest feeling that they were on the way to becoming friends. Or, at the very least, trusting teammates.

Juniper's heart thudded with nerves. She walked toward her dad. She looked up at him, expecting his usual words: *I'm counting on you.*

But when he looked back at her, the deep frown lines weren't there.

He put his arm around her. "The most important thing," he said, "is for you to have a fun time out there, Junebug. I mean . . . you know . . . besides winning the game."

Juniper laughed. "Sure, Dad," she said. She thought that maybe he'd finally changed, just a little. A little was enough for now.

"And I'm so sorry if I forgot that," he continued, giving her a side-armed hug. "I'm going to try harder. I'm proud of you. No matter what."

Juniper felt the bubble of worry burst inside of her. In its place was hope—excitement, even. She suddenly couldn't wait to get out there on the court. Juniper checked in at the scorer's table.

The whistle blew.

Juniper tossed the ball in from the side of the court. It landed in Sarah's hands. Sarah passed it to Mila. Mila tossed it back to Juniper, who was posted up near the basket.

Juniper turned and jumped high.

She used the long length of her arms to shoot above everyone else, even the Warriors' number fifteen. The ball flicked off the tips of her fingertips with the exact right rotation and angle. The ball dropped into the basket.

It's just physics, Juniper thought. She smiled.

The crowd cheered as the Panthers and Warriors ran back down the court. Juniper felt like she was flying.

The Warriors point guard drove the ball down and passed to number fifteen. Juniper was right there, in her face. The tall girl's arms reached above everyone else's except for Juniper's. When the tall girl jumped to shoot, Juniper blocked the shot. Mila managed to grab it from the cluster of ponytails.

Juniper sprinted down the court on offense. She cut toward the basket, wide open. Mila spotted her and hurled the ball toward her.

Juniper had the strangest feeling of deja vu. There she was, all alone, beneath the basket.

The ball was in her hands. The basket was above her. Could she make the shot? Or would she choke?

The other players were still flying down the court. Juniper forgot all about angles and physics and rotation theories. She forgot about music and about everyone else playing their part.

She looked up at the basket and let the instinct take over.

The hours of practice flowed through her arms and down her fingertips. She reached up and up. She let the ball fly from her fingertips.

And it worked.

The ball flew through the net.

Swish!

Mila gave Juniper a high five as they hustled back down the court. The rhythm of the game continued. This time Juniper was a part of it all. Both teams fought hard and went back and forth. The Warriors would surge ahead, and the Panthers would catch up.

It came down to the final minute. The Warriors got a basket to take the lead, 40-38. The Panthers took possession. They passed it around, looking to score.

Time ticked away. Thirty seconds dwindled to twenty. Then down into the teens.

Mila drove in from the wing, but a Warriors guard batted the ball loose. Juniper grabbed the ball near the free throw line. She saw a path and took a dribble toward the basket. Just as she went to shoot, number fifteen drove into her body.

Juniper's shot made it into the air as the ref whistled for a foul. The ball managed to hit the rim and bounce twice. Somehow, it fell in. Tie game. And now Juniper would be shooting a free throw. Her dad jumped up and down on the sidelines in excitement. The fans were making a racket. The Warriors called for a timeout to put extra pressure on Juniper.

There were only ten seconds left.

Juniper walked toward her dad, who gestured for the girls to hustle in.

Juniper thought about all the other games in their season. About her dad yelling at her and singling her out. She thought about all of the bad things that could happen right at this moment. She could choke on her free throw attempt. She could feel like it was all her fault if they lost.

The girls crowded around their coach.

He beamed down at them all. "Well, we've made it this far," he said. "Let's bring this thing home."

The girls smiled up at him. They toweled away sweat and took sips of water. Juniper felt some relief start to flow through her. Mila stood next to her, the top of her head barely reaching Juniper's shoulder. Juniper stood tall and felt some satisfaction at being able to see over everyone's heads. Being tall was who she was. She might as well try to enjoy it.

"You don't have anything left to prove," said her dad. He looked pointedly at his daughter.

He then put his large hand in the middle, and they piled theirs on top of his. Veronica was standing there too, on crutches, her ankle wrapped in a beige bandage. She placed her hand on top of Juniper's.

"Well, there is one more thing I need to say," he said. He had a mischievous look on his face. Juniper held her breath. "Let's win this thing!"

They all cheered.

Juniper didn't know if she would make her free throw or not. She looked at each of her teammates. They were all grinning at her and at each other.

Even Veronica.

Juniper realized it didn't matter what happened. The Panthers were a team. They might win. They might lose. No matter what, they were in it together.

Juniper Jackson stood at the free throw line, her palms slick with sweat. The crowd in her school's gymnasium was silent, waiting.

It was up to her.

GLOSSARY

accusation (ak-yoo-ZAY-shuhn)—a claim that someone has done something wrong

aggressive (uh-GREH-siv)—ready to attack

contagious (kun-TAY-jus)—spreadable

crescendo (kruh-SHEN-doh)—something, like music, that increases gradually the reach the highest point

deflection (de-FLEK-shuhn)—causing something to change direction

demotion (de-MO-shuhn)—to change the rank or position of someone to a lower or less important one

enthusiasm (en-THOO-zee-az-uhm)—great excitement or interest

equation (i-KWAY-zhuhn)—a mathematical or scientific statement

ferocious (fuh-ROH-shuhs)—fierce and savage

humiliation (hyoo-MIL-ee-ay-shuhn)—a feeling of being very ashamed or foolish

offense (AW-fenss)—the way that players on a team try to score points or goals against an opponent

strategy (STRAT-uh-jee)—a careful plan or method

suspension (sus-PEN-shuhn)—the act of forcing someone to not participate as a form of punishment

unruly (un-ROO-lee)—difficult to control

zone (ZOHN)—a type of defense where players guard a certain area (rather than player) on the court

DISCUSSION QUESTIONS

1. At first, Juniper is self-conscious about her height. What happened in the story to change her mind?

2. Juniper's dad is hard on her early in the story. In your opinion, does he act this way more because she's his daughter, or because he wishes he could have played basketball in seventh grade? Explain your answer.

3. Is there someone who is hard on you? If so, why do you think that is?

WRITING PROMPTS

1. Add a scene to the end of the story. Do you think Juniper makes her free throws or not?

2. Think of a time you've had a conflict with a parent or authority figure. Write a short essay about your conflict, explaining what happened and how it was resolved.

3. Write a poem about basketball that uses science or math terms such as *angle, theory, formula, experiment, trajectory*, and so on.

MORE ABOUT . . .
TALL BASKETBALL PLAYERS

The tallest player ever in the Women's National Basketball Association (WNBA) was Margo Dydek. She stood 7-foot-2. She was born in Poland and played center from 1998–2008 for four different WNBA teams.

The average height of National Basketball Association (NBA) players has risen over time. In the 1950s, the average NBA player stood 6-foot-3. In 2018, the average NBA player is a towering 6-foot-8.